CYNTHIA RYLANT

Mr. Putter & Tabby
Smell the Roses

Illustrated by

ARTHUR HOWARD

Houghton Mifflin Harcourt

Boston   New York

For Michael, Laura, Lily, Oliver, and Lula
—A.H.

Text copyright © 2015 by Cynthia Rylant
Illustrations copyright © 2015 by Arthur Howard

www.hmhco.com

The illustrations in this book were done in pencil, watercolor,
and gouache on 250-gram cotton rag paper.
The text type was set in Berkeley Old Style Book.
The display type was set in Artcraft.

Library of Congress Cataloging-in-Publication Data
Rylant, Cynthia.
Mr. Putter & Tabby smell the roses / Cynthia Rylant & Arthur Howard.
pages cm
Summary: When Mr. Putter and Tabby take Mrs. Teaberry to the
Conservatory for her birthday,
Zeke tries his best to stay out of trouble,
but one of the trees is irresistible.
ISBN 978-0-15-206081-7
[1. Birthdays—Fiction. 2. Conservatories—Fiction.
3. Cats—Fiction. 4. Dogs—Fiction.]
I. Howard, Arthur, illustrator. II. Title.
III. Title: Mr. Putter and Tabby smell the roses.
PZ7.R982Mubh 2015
[E]—dc23
2014038080

Manufactured in USA
PHX 3 5 7 9 10 8 6 4
4500568512

1

Together

Mr. Putter and his fine cat, Tabby,
lived next door to Mrs. Teaberry
and her good dog, Zeke.
They all did many things together.
Mr. Putter and Mrs. Teaberry
took walks together
and read books together
and made tea together.

Tabby and Zeke did everything
Mr. Putter and Mrs. Teaberry did,
except sometimes Zeke did it the hard way.

Mr. Putter and Mrs. Teaberry
also celebrated together.
They celebrated Halloween and Christmas
and the first day of baseball season.

They celebrated new tires.

They celebrated good teeth.

And, of course, they celebrated birthdays.

2

Something Special

"Mrs. Teaberry's birthday is on Saturday,"
Mr. Putter told Tabby one morning.
"I want to do something special for her."
All morning Mr. Putter thought of special things
he could do for Mrs. Teaberry.

He thought of ice cream.

He thought of cake.

He thought of balloons.

But they had always celebrated
with those things.

Mr. Putter wanted to do something
extra special this year.

"And besides," he said to Tabby, "don't forget what Zeke does when balloons are in the room."

Mr. Putter made a cup of cocoa
and poured Tabby some cream.
Then he sat in his chair to think.
"I've got it!" said Mr. Putter at last.
It had taken three cups of cocoa,
but he had it!

He would take Mrs. Teaberry
to the Conservatory.
The Conservatory had the most beautiful trees
and plants and flowers in town.
And Mrs. Teaberry loved beautiful trees
and plants and flowers.
She was always telling Mr. Putter
about her maples and her roses.

"Mrs. Teaberry will love the Conservatory,"
Mr. Putter told Tabby.
Mrs. Teaberry's birthday would be good.
It would be special.
"It will be heavenly," said Mr. Putter.

3

Heavenly

On Saturday, Mr. Putter put on
his best shirt and his best tie.
He also put some pomade in his hair.
It made him look very spiffy.
"Pomade makes the man,"
Mr. Putter told Tabby.

Mr. Putter and Tabby knocked
on Mrs. Teaberry's door.
"Happy birthday!" said Mr. Putter.
Mrs. Teaberry was wearing her dress
with all the ruffles and her zebra earrings.
"You look very nice," said Mr. Putter.

Zeke looked very nice too.

His jacket matched the earrings.

"Shall we go?" asked Mr. Putter.

"I can't wait!" said Mrs. Teaberry.

And off they went.

Soon they arrived at the Conservatory.
It was very large.
It had beautiful windows
and beautiful things growing inside.
It was heavenly.

Mr. Putter sniffed the air.
It smelled all wet and flowery.
It reminded him of going outside
in the rain when he was a boy.
It smelled so green.

Mr. Putter and Tabby
and Mrs. Teaberry and Zeke
walked among the trees
and plants and flowers.
They touched the leaves.

They smelled the roses.

They learned the facts.

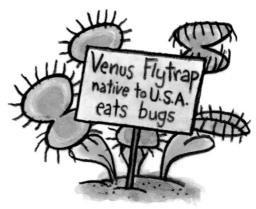

Venus Flytrap
native to U.S.A.
eats bugs

Mr. Putter had told Zeke that if he was
very, very good at the Conservatory,
he might get a surprise.
Zeke lived for surprises.
So he was very, very good.
He was not chewing.
He was not digging.
He was being as good as good can be.

And he stayed that way
for exactly five minutes.

Orchid

Then he found
the banana tree.

BANANA

4

Not So Heavenly

Zeke thought the banana tree was for him.

Zeke *loved* bananas.

He thought the banana tree was his surprise.

So he jumped up and grabbed a bunch,

which made the guard
blow his whistle,
which made Tabby jump
into a lemon tree,

which made lemons hit everybody on the head,
which made the Conservatory not so heavenly!

5

Surprise!

Mr. Putter and Tabby
and Mrs. Teaberry and Zeke
and two bunches of bananas
and nine lemons got into
Mr. Putter's car.

"That was fun!" said Mrs. Teaberry.

"You had fun?" asked Mr. Putter.

"Of course!" said Mrs. Teaberry. "Didn't you?"

Mr. Putter looked at Mrs. Teaberry.
She had a head full of leaves
and a lap full of fruit.
She was such a good sport.
Mr. Putter wanted to keep
giving her special things.
So he drove her to their
favorite ice cream parlor.

They ate lots of strawberry cake
and lots of strawberry ice cream,
and Mr. Putter blew up fifteen balloons.
Mr. Putter looked at Zeke.
Zeke looked at Mr. Putter.
Then Zeke gave Mr. Putter a surprise.

Zeke gave Mr. Putter a *good* Zeke.
There were fifteen balloons in the room,
and Zeke was *good!*

Mr. Putter was so happy that he sang
the "Happy Birthday" song twice.
It was one of the best celebrations ever!
Everyone went home very happy.
Mrs. Teaberry felt very special.
And the next day, there was even . . .

lemonade!